WE THREE KINGS

To my three beloved sons
‿G. S.

Atheneum Books for Young Readers

An imprint of Simon & Schuster Children's Publishing Division

1230 Avenue of the Americas

New York, New York 10020

Illustrations copyright © 2007 by Gennady Spirin

Book design by Michael Nelson

The text for this book is set in Locarno Light.

The illustrations for this book are rendered in watercolor and colored pencil.

Manufactured in the United States of America

First Edition

2 4 6 8 10 9 7 5 3 1

LIBRARY OF CONGRESS CATALOGING-IN-PUBLICATION DATA

Spirin, Gennady.

We three kings / illustrated by Gennady Spirin. — 1st ed.

p. cm.

Summary: An illustrated edition of the traditional Christmas song.

ISBN-13: 978-0-689-82114-1

ISBN-10: 0-689-82114-X

1. Carols—Texts. 2. Christmas music. [1. Carols. 2. Christmas music.] I. Title.

PZ8.3.S7597We 2007

[782.42]—dc22

2006008197

WE THREE KINGS

Illustrated by

GENNADY SPIRIN

Atheneum Books for Young Readers
NEW YORK LONDON TORONTO SYDNEY

WE THREE KINGS OF ORIENT ARE;
Bearing gifts we traverse afar,
Field and fountain, moor and mountain,
Following yonder star.

O star of wonder, star of light, Star with royal beauty bright,

Westward leading, still proceeding, Guide us to thy perfect light.

BORN A KING ON BETHLEHEM'S PLAIN

Gold I bring to crown Him again,

King forever, ceasing never,

Over us all to reign.

O star of wonder, star of light, Star with royal beauty bright,

Westward leading, still proceeding, Guide us to thy perfect light.

FRANKINCENSE TO OFFER HAVE I;
Incense owns a Deity nigh;
Prayer and praising, voices raising,
Worshipping God on high.

O star of wonder, star of light, Star with royal beauty bright,

Westward leading, still proceeding, Guide us to thy perfect light.

MYRRH IS MINE, ITS BITTER PERFUME
Breathes a life of gathering gloom;
Sorrowing, sighing, bleeding, dying,
Sealed in the stone cold tomb.

O star of wonder, star of light, Star with royal beauty bright,

Westward leading, still proceeding, Guide us to thy perfect light.

GLORIOUS NOW
behold Him arise;
King and God
and sacrifice;
Alleluia, Alleluia,
Sounds through the earth
and skies.

O star of wonder, star of light, Star with royal beauty bright,

Westward leading, still proceeding, Guide us to thy perfect light.

WE THREE KINGS

John H. Hopkins Jr., 1857

We three kings of O - ri - ent are, Bear-ing gifts we tra - verse a-

far Field and foun-tain, moor and moun-tain, Fol-low-ing yon - der star.

O __ star of won-der, star of light, Star with roy - al beau-ty bright,

West-ward lead- ing, still pro-ceed- ing, Guide us to thy per - fect light.

2. Born a King on Bethlehem's plain
Gold I bring to crown Him again,
King forever, ceasing never,
Over us all to reign.

3. Frankincense to offer have I;
Incense owns a Deity nigh;
Prayer and praising, voices raising,
Worshipping God on high.

4. Myrrh is mine, its bitter perfume
Breathes a life of gathering gloom;
Sorrowing, sighing, bleeding, dying,
Sealed in the stone cold tomb.

5. Glorious now behold Him arise;
King and God and sacrifice;
Alleluia, Alleluia,
Sounds through the earth and skies.